Time Warp

THE END OF THE CENTURY CLUB

ilya

"The philosophy of time bears powerfully on human emotions. Not only do individuals regret the past, they also fear the future, not least because the alleged flow of time seems to be sweeping them toward their deaths, as swimmers are swept toward a waterfall."

Encyclopædia Britannica

Anyone can become a Father,
but it takes someone special to be a Dad.
Thanks, Dad, for always being there.

The END OF THE CENTURY CLUB
BOOK TWO: *TIME WARP*

Copyright @ 1999 ED HILLYER (a.k.a ILYA)

ISBN 1 899866 20 5

Published by Slab-O-Concrete Publications in association with PANIC!
Parts of this book previously appeared in *The End* #1–4.

Slab-O-Concrete: PO Box 148, Hove, BN3 3DQ, UK
mail@slab-o-concrete.demon.co.uk

EDitorial address:
ILYA, The CLUBHOUSE, 24 RIVINGTON STREET, LONDON EC2A 3DU, UK
ilya@mpawson.demon.co.uk

First printing March 1999

Printed in England

During the greater part of the last year working on this book I made a list,
checked it twice, and at the very moment I needed it, of course, misplaced it. So
if I leave anyone out, forgive me. Woods, Carl, the distressingly normal Chris
Webster, Jakey Boy, Geoff ('Cock!'), Andi, Cookie and Nita, Farrukh, Ian
Migraine, Jobbie, Rae, Giulia, Sina, Dez, Philip (the Boys, the Boys), Corinne,
Pete, Erica, Anna, Wend, Ritzy, Mitzi, Megan, Speedy, Fee, Charles H., Mike K.,
Brad and the whole Angoulême massive, Bethy, Cartoon County, the GOSH
gang, Lisa Sprocket 'n' Abstract Dean, Brizzle FP Martin, Craig, Chris, Lorna, Ellie,
Mark, Simon F, Simon Russell, Sarah Montagu, Søren, Si and Su. Thanks one and
all. I wouldn't have made it without your help and encouragement.

A BRIEF HISTORY OF TIME

KALI
***Terror is
Her name,
Death is in
her breath, and
every shaking
step destroys a
world forever.*** Welcome
to the **KALI AGE.**
It seems that when you talk of Indian
divinities there are no absolutes, or perhaps
something is lost in the translation. According to
how you devine the divine (define the Devi),
– differing texts, representations and her many aspects –
Kali is the female personification of Time. But also Death.
And Rebirth. ⓘ The presence of Kali hangs heavy in this book.
Try to avoid the temptation to flick ahead through the story pages
– you may spoil some of the surprises in store. ⓘ
These are the last days – the End Time. Now more than ever, time is of the
essence. ⓘ As Man has evolved, so have our systems for telling time, the
precision of its division. Stood upon the Earth, spinning in space, we look to the
Sun to measure our day... guided by a gnomon on a dial, or short shadow to long
shadow. To keep track of time, early man also logged the phases of the moon, full moon
to full moon equalling one 'moonth' (the etymological root, not a crap pun!). One cycle of
seasons gives us a year, or twelve moons, or one Earth orbit of the Sun. ⓘ ➜➜➜➜➜➜➜➜➜➚

A French reviewer of the first volume in this series described the central characters' motivation for setting up The END OF THE CENTURY CLUB, *"...pour tuer le temps plutot que le bourgeois"* – to kill time rather than the rich! (*Livres Hebdo, 2 Octobre 1998*). But Cabaret Voltaire sang: "Why kill time, when you can kill yourself?" Or should that be the other way around?☉

Maybe ... maybe SOON, we shall all be set free from our chronol prisons. Free at last! If the Millennium bug corrodes the heartless cæsium rods of our genitrons and chronometers, the calendars will crumble til we're all knee-deep in numbers. 60, 60, 24, 28-31, 12, 10, 100, 1000. After all, "What is time, but a mere tyranny?" said Marius Goring, in *A Matter of Life and Death.*☉

"Act, act in the living present," said Longfellow. He was doubtless referring to the oft-quoted Latin maxim – *carpe diem* – 'sieze the day' – a favourite amongst annoying gits. So immediately do they seize, what gets left out is the rest of it, the reasoning – *quad minimum credula postero* – 'and trust as little as possible to the future'.☉

Bang on, says I, banging on. Who knows what tomorrow will bring. So if just-a-minute hand taps you on the shoulder, fob it off. Find the short cuts that take twice as long. Idle...dawdle......luxuriate ....once the time has flown, it never comes back. Make the time and re-take the time to enjoy your favourite pastime...past time...passed time. ☉

"Time for bed," said Zebedee. The sewer-mouth.

Ed the ED. 12:23/18.2.99☉

➔ Since many Suns and moons, we've tried to tame time, using all the elements at one time or another as clock-making devices. The invention of the pendulum helped regulate the passing hours (*tick-tock*), and so the telling progressed, from astrolabe to grandfather, to electric, to quartz (..........); digital, ironically, lacking hands. Equally inhuman, early clocks had neither hands nor faces, just struck the hour (the French for bell – *cloche* – gave us the word 'clock'). Just as church bells (*ding-dong*) used to call in the pious to worship, now the shrill sounds of alarum (*driiiiing*) summon all those enslaved to their living wage. How times change!☉

"Technology allows us to flick through time," said Goldie, possibly thinking of his Discman. But rather than give us greater control over time, it seems the opposite is true. Although we always seek to wrest control of time, we never quite manage it ... sentenced to play catch-up for all eternity – making up for lost time.☉

Working all hours to chronicle more adventures in the final days before this book is due to go to press, how I wish time had a more elastic quality. I daren't lose track of time, since it never loses track of me. How I wish for a less strict regime , rather than the dread finality of deadline, my own miniature apocalypse, as the final hour strikes (*doom...DOOM...**DOOM***).☉

↖The Pyramids of Ancient Egypt signified both Death and Time. Bugger! Now I wish I'd worked THEM into the story somewhere too.

↑*The Four Horsemen of the Apocalypse*, Death, War, Famine and the Other One, from the Cologne Bible, 1479

NO SUCH THING

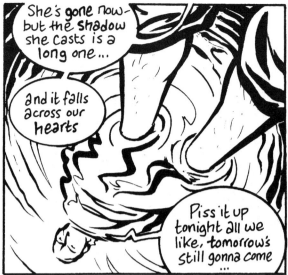

THE
END
is
NiGH

11

It wasn't the right time...

or place. If I ever see her outside the shop, or when it's not so busy...

It's always busy!

I gave her a club flier... you never know...

YOU NEVER!

And don't try and kid me you're sorry

You might still be able to make good your intentions

...next time.

What is it with me and girls behind food counters?

hey man

hey man listen i don't mean to hassle you but

AW, COME OHN! WOULD YOU GO UP TO A DOG WITH IT'S HEAD IN IT'S BOWL 'N' TRY TO PULL IT AWAY?

Huh? WOULD you?

I BEEN A GOOD BOY T'DAY AN' MY HEAD'S IN MY BOWL

SO LEAVE ME ALONE, OKAY!

'Funny thing about money ...there's only so much to go around.

Maybe enough for everyone, maybe not.

'But it doesn't belong to anyone.

'Sometimes I wish I could be more like those people who like to live it large, and just forget...

'There's always someone else...

'Somewhere else...

...who is having to pay the bill for you.

ACCIDENT
• THURSDAY • PM
14/9/93   11·30
CONTACT
PUBLIC EYE PLC

25

Someone like **you**, because you're too good to be **true**

Yeah. Aren't I though.

I gotta swing by my sister's house.. sort some stuff out...

Reckon you'll be here when I get ba

SZZZ NORK

...?

≒ sigh ≒

... the face of an angel ...

... and the undercarriage of the very devil.

Buck

honey

... come back to bed

y'say somethin', Cash?

I don't want you to go ... not now

Th' invitation was for **both** of us, darlin'

But Chaarles ...

O.K., Shoot! No sweat, we'll stay ...

T'ain't lak ah reckon they need us ur nothin'. But mebbe ah should...

Do nothin', my man, but get back in this bed this instant

Since ya put it lak thet ...

Any partick'lar reason for this change o' heart?

I don't like the way that Indian girl looks at you...

Ah don't lak th'way the blond guy with all the dreadlocks looks at me, but don' fret none. Ah c'n handle it

You know you c'n trust me. You know ah love you

do you?

'Semper Fidelis'

...it's the only Holy Roman ah know.

They're good people, Cash. Invitin' me ta join their click. It's the kinda thing ah need

A new direction

'Nude erection' Mmmn

HEY!

... hey

You tell them?

Ain't got no...

What's passed is passed

Ancient ≡ nmh ≡ history

Even so, Buck, better watch your back...

Ah

..the past has a way of catching UP

29

34

'To the park'

= Sigh =
O.K., I give in.
Why have we
hired out
a boat?

WHY are
we sat in the
middle of
this lake?

Tonight's
our big night.
The first
club night!

AND
...

...

well, it
wouldn't be
right to start
off without
due ceremony
...

we're
bonding

oh good
grief

An'
here's
the best
part

WHOO!

Chatte
Papier
Naff

Let's
Bond!

Let's
BOND!

POP

'mazing what
you find in the
DJ booth at
clubs, innit

'part
from records,
obviously

Of course!
Spats is where
Tip won us
that magnum
with her
tampon
that time,
and we
...

= Spfff =

"I'd forgotten all **about** that. We're lucky they didn't remember our faces..."

"Bouncers aren't exactly employed for their brain-power!"

"uh. no offense, BUCK"

=glug=

"Ah never had champagne before"

"Tipple, Tippoo? There's plenty"

"Have some, TIP. It's =hic= luver-ly"

"Poo Tips?"

"Aw, come ohn, TIP..."

"whoa"

=hic=

"TIP"

LUCY

BIG BONE

"WILLIE!"

"...Don't ro..."

TANIA

BIG BONE

WOOARGH

SPALOOSH

41

I don't see why we have to do this

WANKA WANKA WANKA

SPURT PROTEIN WASH FOR ALL YOUR...

I'd rather go home and change

Have a bath

There's no time

..welcome the crowds

We should be back at the club by seven...

VMMM

Anyway, what's your problem?

It's warm enough in here

But my underwear's soaked thru'!

SNAP SNAP

uh huh

you aren't the only one

So, you could've put them in the dryer too, if'n you'd wanted

scary though the concept is...

WHAT?

All our other kit'll be dry soon enough

you c'n get yer knickers off then

..those as can wait that long

43

Stunning. Yah.

Some clothes you can watch an' they appear for maybe five whole turns

but then... they disappear completely!

These aren't ours, y'know

ours went straight in the dryer

I know. Somebodie's service wash

Magic!

Plik

fssh

≡sup≡

If you think about it...

a launderette is like a... a microcosm

The people running it like to keep seperate the whites from the coloureds

≡sniff≡ poo-wee

what was in that water?

WE were, dimbulb

...and the delicates

But, you know, after the inevitable final rinse

we all get hung out to dry in the end

It all comes out in the wash

...

Sometimes I'm so profound, I even impress myself

Silver under-pants!

Kinky

≡slup≡

≈Heh≈ Trust **those two** to find themselves a surrogate television

Better programmes too, I'll wager

PAT PAT

WONG

Aren't they dry yet?

Nope

VMM

I'm bored now

And my bum's getting numb

Too bad not **everyone's** as easily diverted

Sorry...

..But I just don't happen to have any playing cards or amusing board-games on me right now

PAT PAT

...unless you fancy a game of snakes and ladders!

Hey!

Of course, in the old days...

before they invented T.V...

..Folk had to make their own fun

Sure'n' why don't you pull out that grand piano an' we'll gather 'round it for a sing-song

I'll tell you what we could **play**

uh-oh

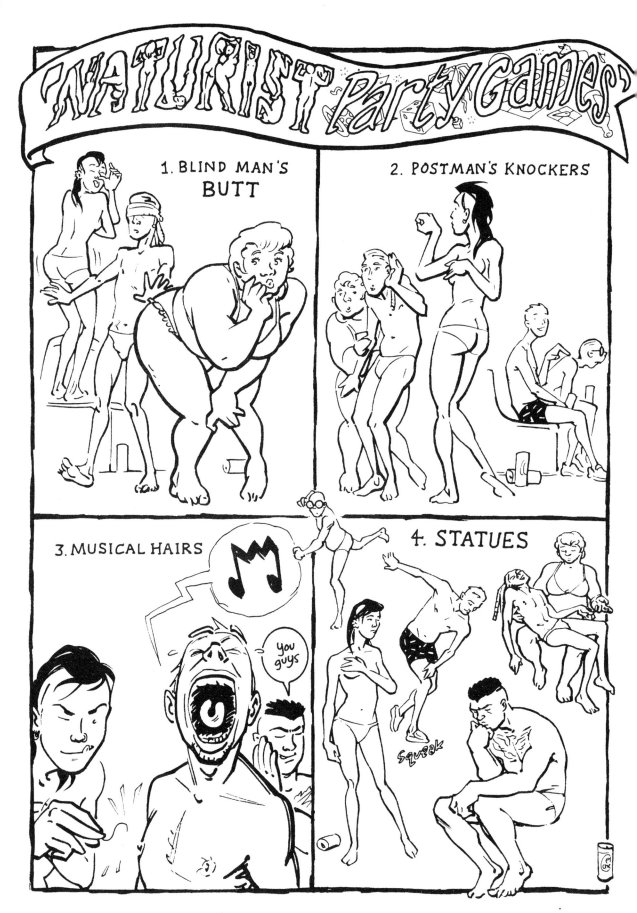

49

I'm not mad keen on all these balloons..

hFF

..looks like it's a kiddie's tea-party or somethin' ...

They'll have to do...

..at least until we can afford to fix the gestapo lighting.. organise something a shade more... sultry.

≡Tut≡

You've got beautiful bone structure

..For an American, I mean

Most of the ones you see on telly an'shit look so.. bland

... blonde

You look a lot like my first boyfriend... exceptin' of course he was black

Oop, careful! Nearly had your eye out then.. Keep still!

mah... bloodline is a little crazy mixed-up

... SIR?

'CHARLES'?

BUCK?

Shouldn't that be 'CHUCK'?

Your young lady's been ringing most of de afternoon ...

Sounds more than a little upset, if yez ask me. Says to 'Tell charlie I need him at home'

oh

ah'm much obliged to ya

Ah'm sorry. Bill

BUUUCK! What if there's

That's O.K. BUCK Go where you're needed

I hope everything's alright

Let him go

It's not like there's much call for CROWD CONTROL here right now, is there?

You know, he's a handsome looking fella, that one

Polite too

grunt

Say, Geronimo. When's the party startin'?

It'll happen

54

JUMP AROUND JUMP JUMP

What's that meant to be?

Runes, innit

Ancient Celtic good luck charm

fffft

FFFt

Hey Wow, she looks grreat!

You're a dab hand at this, sis!

I am, aren't I

Let me see, let me see!

ooh

Where did all these face-paints come from...?

GROWL!

Prr

?

Some place in the arcade, what does it....

You had this all planned out, that's the point of it...

You cook up all these grand schemes and it doesn't even ever occur to you to let anybody else in on it

..any of the poor sods involved

We're just pawns in your game yet again

Now this...

This is a good idea

If only you'd stuck with the face-painting and left it there

Sure an' I could've done without the rest of your ceremony — or at least some warning of it

RAWR! ≈ffsst≈

eep

Led around like a prize goose, dunked in the boating lake, a happy hour buck naked an' freezin' in full view of the entire neighbourhood

DAH HA HA — HOO HOO HA HA

..an' these jeans're killing me

'BUCK, NAKED'

Let's cherish that thought for a moment, shall we?

...ARGH, you're impossible!

What's that all over your...

What the hell you got on..?

We, uh, we fell in th' water, then we...we swopped outfits. It's a long story...

PUSSY POWER

How'd ya lak mah new pants?

Drop your trousers and I'll tell you

RIIIIP!

Hey

Ah thought you were meant t'be all upset

'.. A HANDFUL OF UNDERAGE DRINKERS, LONESOME LOSERS, AND A BUNCH OF SOAP-DODGING, FREE-LOADING LUNCH-OUTS WHO'VE PROBABLY SMUGGLED IN THEIR OWN BEER ...'

That's what you wanted, isn't it?

'a club for people like us'?

Ooh. look what the cat dragged in

The heavies

BANG!

OW!

OY

OW

YOU'RE MEANT TO PAY!

EAMONN

WHERE ARE YOU, IDJIT?

IVY! What a pleasure. How are you, love, how's business?

DON'T GIVE ME ANY O'YER SOFT SOAP

WHAT IS IT YOU'RE TRYIN' T'PULL? I'VE TOLD THEM BEFORE ABOUT LITTERING UP MY PUB WITH YOUR HANDBILLS!

I don't know what...

THEY'VE BEEN DOIN' IT AGAIN - LOOK!

IT'S £3. YOU'RE MEANT TO..

HERE'S ONE OF THE WEE SHITES NOW

PUB

RRK!

It's crap here. No atmos

At least the music's good...

I KNEW IT!

Studley Dudley?

DUUDE How're y'doin?

YOU STOLE MY RECORDS YOU SNEAKY SHIT!

DDDJ

DUDLEY!?

D'YOU WANNA, uh, PLAY A SET?

Shit

AN'A PACKET OF CRISPS, I SAID

...CUNT

What Flavour?

...TOSSER

C'mon, cash, a night out'll do ya good

I don't know, BUCK

Ah wish you'd tell me what's spooked ya...

OAF

COW

HARRIDAN

WEASEL

ah!

Hang the D.J.

65

67

FUCK YOU
I WAITED HALF
THE NEXT DAY FOR
YOU TO TURN
UP. THANKS A
BUNCH

DEATH

..Twelve.. Thirteen! Not bad for one hour

This really works!

Like taking candy...

HOMELESS PLEASE HE

All the better for us lookin' all beat up, after our opening 'bash'

One look at our obvious plight

...they can't help but dig deep

I wanna take a break ...I can buy my own fags now, huh

...

...maybe later...

I wonder if it would work even better with you on your own...

'the abused and single young mum'...

YOU AIN'T LEAVIN' ME TO DO THIS ALONE JUST COS' YOU'RE BORED WITH IT..!

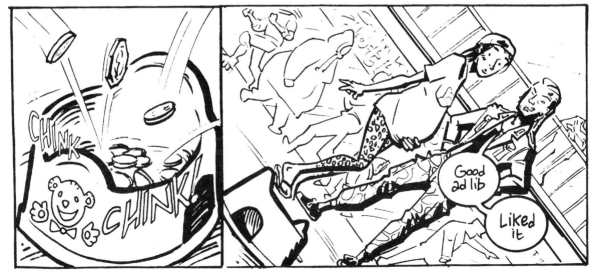

CHINK

CHINK!

Good ad lib

Liked it

SPREAD THOSE CHEEKS, KIDS, **DADDY'S** HOME!

...what's eating you?

BLC's plotting his revenge

car driver tried to kill him

So what else is new

An' he saw a real big pile-up with lots of dead bodies 'n' blood 'n' brains 'n' everything!

TIP not here?

Not since this morning

Really weird thing, right. We were up the precinct when all of a sudden she just disappears

I thought she must've come back here

Who's 'Sulliman'?

Prob'ly one of her boyfriends. It's kind of hard to keep track

...I think that's what she shouted when she scarpered...

Even when she's brought one of 'em home, she's not that big on introductions

What were you doing in the precinct?

...

uh...

I found a pubic hair in the margerine again this morning

Bless you

Honey..spread... that time we found her gaffa taped to the mattress...

Time was she was made of stone... wouldn't look at anyone

Nowadays it's anything in trousers. Not that it's improved her general mood any

It's just a phase, I'm sure

...I hope

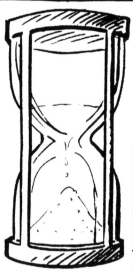

OY!

WHO'S BEEN EATING ALL THE EGGS?!

eh?

EH?

Boy racer...

Thinks he can go 'round...

...treating everyone like...

PARASITES

Jeez, calm down, TIP!

I'll only be gone a couple of hours at the most...

I can't unarrange it. Barney's expecting me!

You've got to face up to your responsibilities ...it's your baby too.

Why are you so...

?

Why are you so irritable and jumpy this morning? You can take this rôle-playing thing too far you know

Is it something to do with that 'SULLIMAN' episode from yesterday?

SULEIMAN

Well, who is he? What is he?

Tell me

... then over here I want to put some runner beans

I just wish the soil could be deep enough for carrots

Y'all got ya self a reg'lar truck patch. Ah'm impressed

Collard greens are mah favorite, with a pepper sauce ..mm, mm

...

Ah guess it's jest a Southern thing

Ah hope ya don't mind me asking, Miss Diane...

Miss Daisy

What?

uh... Deeanne. It's Deanne

Just Deanne

?

... What the heck happened here? ...looks laik a bomb hit it.

You could say that

'Folk are worth more than that. We're not dogs.'

You **BULL-SHITTER!**

All that toss about pride, and now look at you!

And look at her...

≈SPFFF≈

rattle rattle

CHINK

I guess old habits do die hard, huh?

Funny. I hadn't noticed before...

That girl in the bagel shop, reminds me of TIPPOO

Wha...

I don't

CHINK on pie hel

Despite appearances, we're not squatters

I bought this house with my ex-husband

or at least, we were in the process of doing it up and paying off the mortgage when we split up

oh, ah'm sorry

oh, that's ok. It's not important

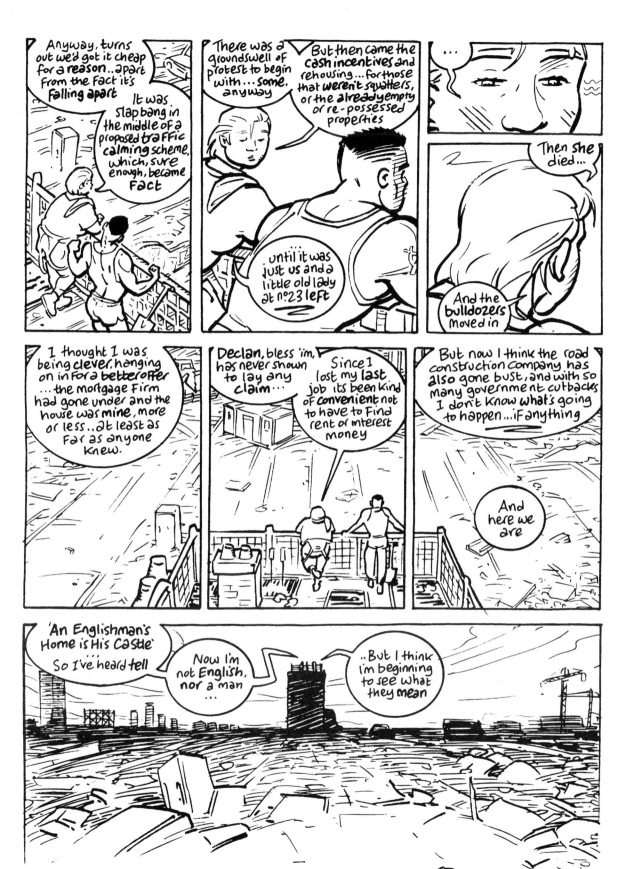

OIII!! GE'A BLOODY MOOVE ON, YOU LOT!

GERVAISE!

BABOOSHKA!

HONK

ova 'ere, NAH!

BWAH HA HA HA HA HA

Asia

Barry Larry?

Surinder

Wesley. Wez

I've always liked wesley

Frankie!

How is... Cashmere, is it?

Tell her I'm sorry about the other night

... we all are

Oh. She's O.K. She doesn't mean ta be unfriendly.

She jest a homebody, is all

Got somethin' on her mind, too. Ah don't know whut...

Well, i'm just glad you arrived when you did

To even up the odds

Still an'all, we were lucky

... lucky the turnout was so low, given the night ended with sucha huge barney!

Now he's set up some kind of **Nostalgia** shop over there and wants it all shipped back. But my Dad said we threw it all out. He doesn't like Bradley.

Here it is. Got a puncture. Should be alright.

What you want it for, anyway?

You'll find out

I want it back if it's worth anything

Barn, you said your Dad was in the war...

The Falklands ConFlick, yeh.

And he has a thing for militaria, right?

...Does he keep any stuff up here anywhere?

Maybe you were right, honey

SSSSSSS

Deanne says the bar-owner's some kind of a drug addict!

Cash Honey?

SOLDIER OF FORTUNE

PARANOID DELUSION SPECIAL!

BLAZING UP + BIG BREAK

MIX WITH AUTOM

GUNS AND AMMO

IN THIS ISSUE

MIGHT WEAPON FOR...

BINGO!

I need to borrow this, too.

96

DE FAHR HARSEMON OF DE APOCOLLAPSE!

Fred, George, Keith and Brian

I am not going to have quads

DEAT'

WAH

FAMIN'

Rita

Oliver

THE END IS NIGH

DE FAHR HARSE MON

DEY COMIN'

Since when has **debt** been one of the Four Horsemen?

Look at all these suits. I never thought of there being **three** rush hours in a day

A lunch-time rush. How can they stand it...?

THE END IS SAY!

Still... good for business!

Have I told you the parable of the travelling salesman?

OK, to be good at his job, right, this travelling salesman must find the quickest route from A to B.

Which he does ...

But he doesn't get to relax in the extra time he's gained ...

time he's gained ...

Instead, he uses it to scramble for C, and get there sooner

97

≡Sigh≡

What day is it? Wednesday? Let's try the market

CRUNCH

CHECK IT!

Aidan

No!

Amerjit, then

Since when did we decide it was going to be a boy, anyway

You wouldn't rather it was a boy?

That's kind of an issue for me

What do you ...?

I'd rather not talk about it.

...ambulance came before I could prise it from her cold dead fingers

She was dead?!

Figure of speech

BLAT

OW!

HOMELESS Please HELP

WHAT ON EARTH DID YOU THINK YOU WERE DOING?

YOU'RE NOT HOMELESS!

I live in a van. I think that counts!

YOU ABOVE ALL SHOULD KNOW BETTER...

Ah have always relied on the kindness of strangers

BLAT

An' I thought you said you weren't in the club

Oh shut it

...folk find out they're being taken for a ride, it makes it that much harder on the truly deserving

Next time someone in real need approaches them for help, they'll think twice

And you. You shouldn't be encouraging him!

egging him on

Talking of which...

URK

I believe you've got some explaining to do!

103

y'doing great kid. Ya godd'em on da ropes. Dey don'know which way ta toin

DINGO
DINGO

We can't run a club on air

And we wouldn't have to pull any cushion scam IF you would release some funds from that cashbox you've hidden

We've been through that and we all agreed. As the door money from a gig that got broken up we should give it back to the band concerned. All of it.

Duh

I have actually been concious the last month or two. Tell me something I don't know

I was re-iterating for the benefit of those who may not have been present and are not aware of the full ramifications

If I can fix a meet with someone from N.W.O, will you hand over the cashbox then?

Maybe

'Maybe'?!

Well, yes of course. IF I can trust you

Just promise me you won't take Tip out begging again

Cross my heart

You know what's the best contraceptive in the whole world?

children

yeh, but they slip off easily when you really get going

you're sick!

ohhh, my achin' back. your turn tomorrow

Now I can't really see that working, can you?

Having me, not you, in the family way

whatever. I've had enough for today.

SCHLOOP

Best get these back home to Dee, before she lays one

She gave me the money this morning

Oo. Not free range. she won't like th

GREY!

Cool! wait for me, I won't be a second

O.K.

GREY!

Hold up a moment, geezer

A word in your shell-like...

109

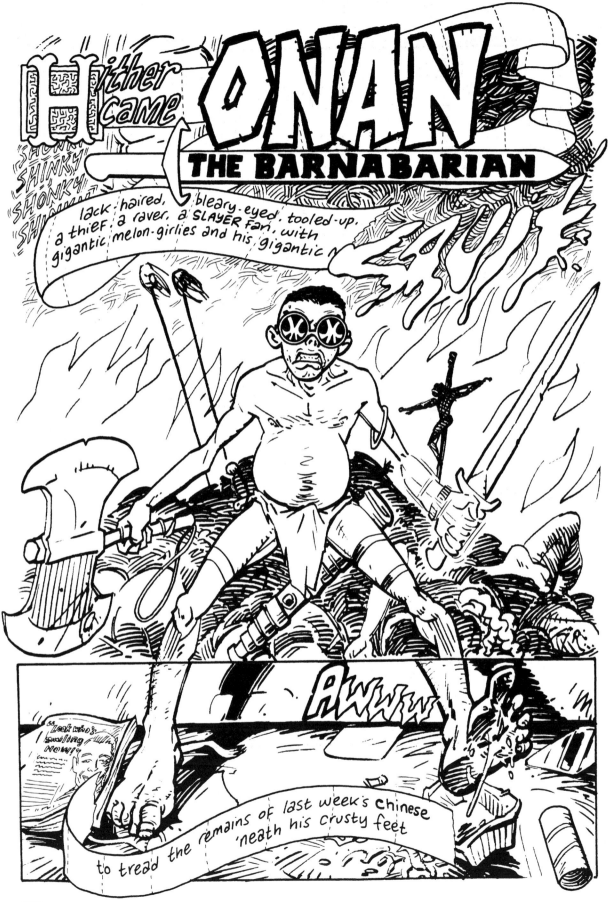

Come in, My Sons!

By God, you make an old man extremely proud, and not only that, a very happy Man, also.

HAHA!

‹Thank you, Dalgeet›

CLIK

‹How are you, my fair one?›

‹It ... is a long time, since you have called me that.›

‹It is a long time since you have been that›

< You look lovely in that *Kameez*>

< But oh my child, what have you done with your hair!>

< It is the way I like it>

< Your **Father** has a lot of hope and ambition for you. You must try to live up to his faith in you and fulfil his life's wishes>

< Yes. Afterall, he has so much invested in me>

...and told him to get himself stuffed!

<Nadir>

He was shaking like a bloody leaf, I tell you

<May I speak with you?>

<Of course my love, speak.>

<No, Nadir. We must talk>

You've never told me how you met TIP in the first place

Sorry, WHAT?

I said you never have told me how you met TIP...

I mean given that she's virtually adopted now

'adopted'?!

Yeah, one of your waifs and strays, Deanne...

...like we all are one way or another

...

I met her in a nightclub, funnily enough

That would be shortly after Declan left, then, when you were

seeking reassurance

Let's put it like that, shall we?

... when I was foolish enough to think life would be incomplete without a man

Nothing foolish!

It was sad... tragic, even. She was just fresh off the bus, looking to pick up men just so she'd have a place to stay.

Luckily I caught her in time

Time to what? Hasn't stopped her any since, picking up men

I'm sure she has her reasons

Same as mine, perhaps

I doubt it

OK, alright, you brought BIC to me when he needed a roof, but there's no way I'm letting BARNEY...

117

So the SINGHs're going on a family outing, right— He's got his two brothers and their wives in the boot

His wife, her sister and eight kids wedged in the back seat

His mother and three more kids squashed in the front

an' his wife's 70 year old parents strapped to the roof rack with the luggage

The car gets about 300 yards and collapses

'Oh dhir me', says Mr. Singh, 'It is my wife's case that is doing it'

'She is having ever such a lot of jewellery'

 BWAH HAH HAH

Well I thought it was funny

My Dad says them Muslims, they're fundamentalist nutters

What do you say?

I said, my Dad says, them Muslims No, no I meant

Oh forget it. That's probably the most honest answer I could hope for

Anyway, Tippoo's lot aren't Muslims. At least I don't think they are.

I think they're Hindus. Whatever that means

One thing's for sure. They're a bunch of PAKis

Don't talk ignorant. I'm not sure where in India they come from

And she was born here. So what does that make her?

Let's face it, immigrants do make the place slummy, 'cause in their own countries they don't live the same as us. They eat different food and everyfink and it must smell.

An' they do different things like the way they put their rubbish out an' all that

What, like not out of their mouths you mean?

DAMN. I really wish I'd been here. I would've like to've had the chance to go with them

Rescue her

Better than sitting around here listening to you parrot your rubbish

'You're rubbish'

119

120

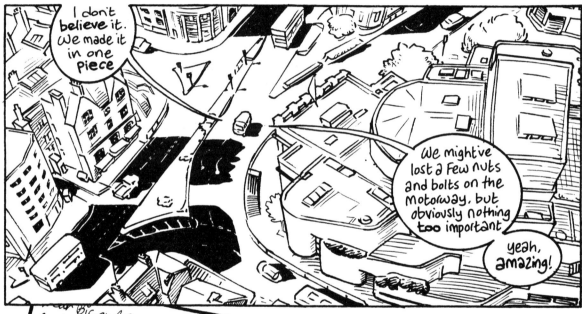

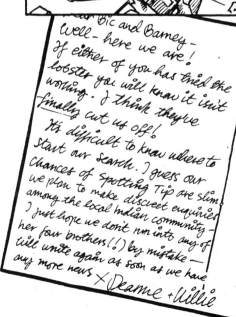

≈gloan≈

Wish I was at home. At least where I'm normally parked, a fellow can rub shoulders with the sheets until mid-day like a CIVILIZED gentleman

grumbly mumbly!

NEW TIME IN COMIC-BOOK FORM!

CONAN THE BARBARIAN

TO THE DEATH!

E 150

COMING OF CONAN!

DC

The money din't yours, so kiss your playboy dreams or whatever they are goodbye

≈pfft≈

WAILING WALL

PFFT

Sigh

HEY FANBOY YOU CAN LOOK ALL YOU WANT BUT DON'T TOUCH!!

KEEP ALL LIMBS BEHIND THE BARRIER

THIS MEANS YOU

OR 'SNIKT!

Poof

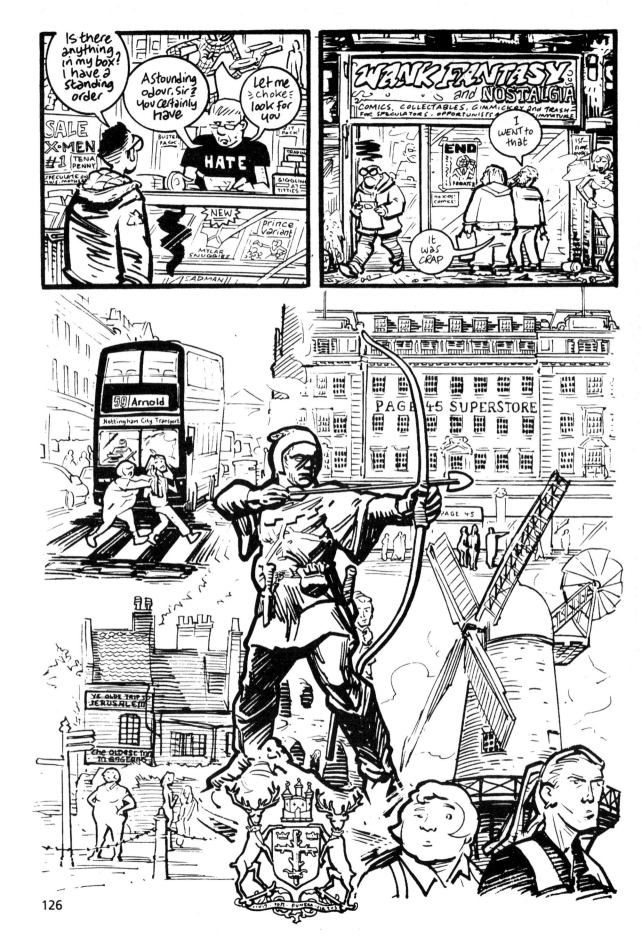

127

What do you think they're doing?

Preparations for the big day, I guess. Checkin' everythings sorted

Don't talk much, do they

Tip said they don't when they're together...

...like they're psychic or something

says it's creepy

I can see that

Spooky buncha 'c' words

Four brothers, eh? What are the chances of that?

You're forgetting our cousins on Da's side

Auntie Mary's fourth child after three boys in a row was the girl she'd been trying for all along—

only it was stillborn, poor thing

Their fourth boy John has never got over the notion that maybe he wasn't wanted

Who does, when your upbringing's Catholic

< You can drive an express train through a girl who has known so many men >

< A cheap tart >

Tht tht

< Your tongue will come out in boils if you continue to talk about your sister like that >

< I was only repeating something I heard uncleji say >

< What does your uncle know!? >

More English than you, old woman!

129

132

RRRRMMM

OMAR 1

OMAR! My good friend

<Suleiman, it is good that you could come>

<It is an honour, Nadir, to have been invited>

I owe you a debt of thanks, Sherif, for this wonderful day you have made possible

Psh! It is a simple matter...

...the sharing of information

How is your tigress?

Tamed

GET ALL THESE GIGGLING IDIOTS AWAY FROM ME!!

KLANG!

GEK

And your sons...

They did a splendid job. They should come and work for me

HA HA

HA HA

133

With respect Subaji, why are you telling me this?

ONI is eldest

RAVI

We both know who it is has inherited his Father's strength

...and who, his brains

< The day goes well but you are not glad, My wife >

our guests lack the sunshine of your smile

< The commission of that bandit and his intrusion into our affairs...>

<...unseemly haste in the fixture of this ceremony, in which we lose our only daughter...>

< ... My blessing did not matter on either of these occasions...>

< Why should it now? >

< Suleiman Omar has done us a great favour. He is a man of honour >

< I will not hear you speak ill of him >

< Long since has this union been agreed >

< Ritu was promised Tippoo for his wife when he was but a child ...>

< and my dear.. he is only in this wretched country most temporarily! >

< SHE HAS NO LOVE FOR RITU! >

< She will learn to find it, as you found love for me... and I, for you >

< I fear your concern for the future happiness of our beloved is less than your desire to cement an arrangement >

< The partnership whose success you anticipate the most eagerly of all, is that between your business... and that of the father of Ritu >

Wait ...

ah!

There

136

< IF you love your daughter, I beg of you ... >

< It is too late >

< There will be no better offer >

< Nobody will marry second-hand girls >

< You have a lump of cut quartz for a heart >

Dalgeet!?

< Ah, mistress. I have been looking al—

< Why are you not with TIPPOO? >

< It's almost ≋ hhh ≋

< Tell me you did not leave her alone... >

?

< ...I locked the... >

TIPPOO!

TIPPOO!

Rattle!

AYAH!

Buh hur

Buh huu huuh

Tip?

Hush now, hushhh. What's the matter?

What is it?

I'M STILL A VIRGIN!

WAAAHHHH

ehhhhh

...hold on. You're ...

What're you saying? All the guys you.. uh, go with

...and excuse me there's been more than a few of them ...

...are you telling me that you don't actually sleep with them?

145

A gypsy once told me my days were numbered

29 30

Full Moon

PARTY

When I got home I looked at the wall calendar and saw that it was true

...DEADLINE LOOMING EVER LARGER, THE GOVERNMENT HAS. TO DATE, SPENT AN ESTIMATED TWO BILLION POUNDS INVESTMENT IN A NATIONAL MONUMENT FOR THE NEW CENTURY

A PROJECT CURRENTLY UNDER CONSTRUCTION ON THE SOUTH BANK OF THE THAMES NEAR TO THE GREENWICH MERIDIAN, AND SURROUNDED ... BY CONTROVERSY

148

150

151

152

Any spare change for the needy

Big Issue, mistah?

THIS WEEKS COMICS

F.P

Can you spare £3?

'Three...? Are you kidding?

£3 Jeez'is. You can tell we're uptown

£2

I'll get on my knees for £2!

...But none of them offered as little as that for my time.

I've had men dressed much smarter than you say that to me before now

Hey, no, STOP IT. You don't have to do that

Here look, here's 1.50. I'd give you more but I don't like t'be...

HAH! yer face is as familiar as your M.O.

You're from round our way, aren't ya.

What's y'name?

Neil?

Heh Right

Here's a flyer for my club. Neil

Start saving

161

163

165

Nuh-uh ENGLIAN!

What are you on about now?

She on the blob?

Like we never have moods for any other reason

Well, I mean talk about yer behavioural swings

I tried to explain to Buck how she's just 'Ferociously individual'

... I don't think we've yet met the real Tip

Most of her actions seem to be for the sake of rebellion

'It's like she doesn't know – hasn't been given the chance to know – who she is... what she wants to be. She's yet to find her own voice.'

Her... loose behaviour? I think it's been like a compulsive need to make herself unfit for her Father's wishes...

It's not like she enjoys it. She's said so herself!

'Going from one extreme to another is her trying to assert her independence –she'll balance out eventually... she'll find herself a middle ground.'

Like what? A chastity belt with velcro fasteners?

What did you say?

Oh, we were just wondering how much longer you were going to be hogging the mirror

I'm sorry did I say 'hogging'?

I meant 'fogging'

Puff

Pant

What happened? Did anyone pay?

Nup. We ...did a runner

Food ws.. shit anyway

Kof

oh my god

What were you trying to do – shove her head into the Tampax dispenser?

Yes

Tippoo got into a fight?

DUH

Coupla tarts, they insulted her

Maybe it's the way she's 'dressed'...

...or perhaps it was her charming manner

They're just jealous fat women

No offense

I wasn't

Now, though...

Maybe I'm wrong

Maybe she is just a bitch

Get any sauce on my top and you are dead, Barney

x

168

174

183

'Pretty Lady. This is for you' —compliments of the DJ

Hey. Glad you could make it!

Thanks for saving my bacon the other day—

No problem. Thankyou F'invitin' us

How's the arm?

If you hadn't rolled by when you did...

Hey. don't mention it...Guy woz drivin' like a psycho

an' look who we brought with us ...

GEORGEOUS GEORGE!

Geezer

Who's thet?

George? Owns the valley of Dead Cars

Where them skatey kids hang out..where Willie's van is parked

Which makes him Willie's land..er.. lord, I guess

Funny lookin' fella

errr yup

He's a she or was

YA 58

187

Not bad. Fer a bunch of kids

I never thought the day would come we would be able to fill this place. Thankyou.

No, thank you Petal. Me an' the boys are ever so grateful to ya

...for giving us this chance to recoup some of our losses from the last gig

Hopefully our share of what you make tonight will go towards replacing some of our gear that got impounded, not to mention springing Frank from the bail hostel. He hates it in there

Make sure you thank that angel of a brother of yours from me

Thank him?

I'LL KILL 'IM

'Kinell, Neil!

Not in 'ere, mate

Here

Chill out, fella

Take the night OFF

whoop

That's my cue

THWAP

HOLD IT RIGHT THERE YOU

Not now, Dee

I'M ON

'say something'

'say those words she'd really like to hear'

...the ones you've wanted to say for so long...

W...

...one cream cheese tomato, one egg mayonnaise, and a coke

SHIT!

SHIT SHIT SHIT!

I'm tryin'!

She obviously din't know what I wuz talkin' about

Y'weaselled cashbox offame - tol'me given th'funds to GREY

bu'mustof used 'em t'set up tonight

Y'kept TIP out preggy beggin'

Knowin' I'd know

Knowin' it'd annoy me...

Azza COVER STORY!?

SING

SMAT!

WE COULD'VE BOUGHT THOSE RECORDS ANYTIME!

WE DIN'T NEED TO STEAL

RAAGH!

YOU SCHEMING QUEEN!

Laters Dee

'Nature calls'

olé!

BILL?

BEN!

Darling! =MWAH=

Am I glad to see you...

im gasp-ing!

..I've just got to bum a fag!

ah'm outta here

191

Damn things...

stiff!

AH!

OK, hand 'em over

WILLIAM

O.K— quick!

start feeding me!

I DEMARN A FULL ESKPLANA SHUN

BARN-cover me!

Five

Six

?

Odd...

'Nelssson' must've ssold us one too many

193

194

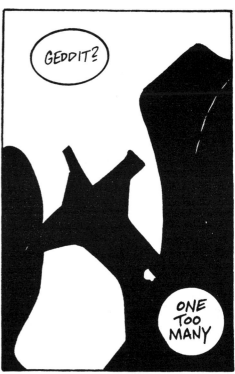

FUCK THIS FOR A GAME OF SOLDIERS
GOODBYE CRUEL WORLD!
NNOOOO
BANG

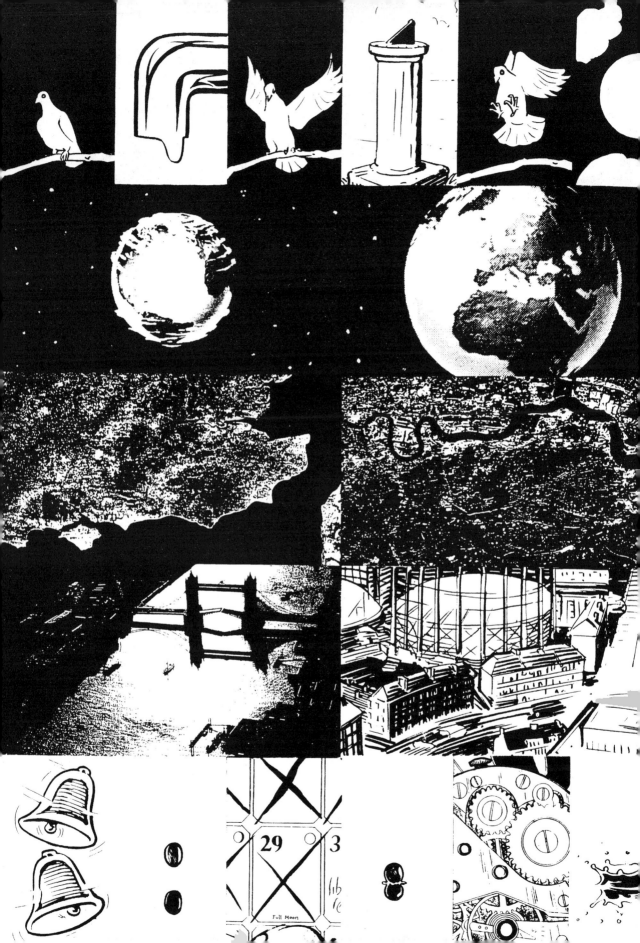

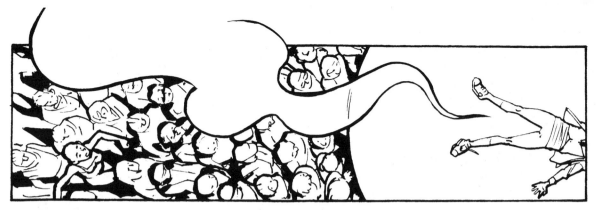

GRRRRA

SOMEBODY GET THIS DAMN DOG OFFA ME!

NO, BARN, IT WAS JUST AN INFLATABLE I GOT FROM WOOLIE'S FOR £2.99

HERE Y'GO. I WAS GONNA USE IT. BUT IT NEEDED PAINTING...

AND WHEN I SAW THE SIZE OF IT. ONCE I'D BLOWN IT UP, WELL, I JUST COULDN'T BE ARSED

— AND IT'S NOT OFTEN YOU'LL HEAR ME SAY THAT!

groan

WILLIE— please stop shouting!

I WAS SHOUTING?

Cant believe it's over already

The WORLD of THE END as we know it

Released a couple of years back, the first volume of *The END OF THE CENTURY CLUB* has, in its own modest way, set the world alight... or at least, set the international comics community to smouldering slightly. Apart from various foreign language features (excerpted below), there was an uncharacteristically rave review in the pages of America's *Comics Journal*. But by far the best thing to happen to me in my entire career so far has been the translation of the book into French!

LA DIFFERENCE

In France, as in much of Europe and the rest of the world, comics are accepted and even celebrated as a valid and valued part of the culture – something still a long way off in England; even in

foreign and something of a commercial longshot. Even so, the print run is immediately double what we can manage – and what's more, the album is a HARDBACK!

French bookshops can return unsold stock up to two years after

anything at all, *Le CLUB de la fin de siècle* should be a success.

French journalists are so refreshing. They actually read the material and take an interest in it. And they discuss it, rather than just regurgitate this week's PR guff'n'bluff, or rehash last weeks articles of same.This past year I've been interviewed at least a couple dozen times. I've been on the radio – usually on tape, but also live in a round table discussion at an Anarchist station in Paris. I've attended signings, drawn live on stage, and most terrifying of all, on television for Canal Plus – wearing make-up, under hot studio lights, with a room full of technicians and producers, other much more veteran comics artists, the cameras rolling and time

America, despite the iconic status of *Superman* and all the rest. My French publisher, Bethy, is a newcomer, and relatively small. My art style and argot (considered *nouvelle vague*, <new wave>) is

publication, so it is still too early to tell how the thing has sold. But if the amount of press attention it has recieved, and the overwhelmingly positive and excited critical reception means

ticking. I was shit, of course.

The most fun of all has been the chance to attend the festivals – Darnétal in Normandy, and the big daddy of them all, Angoulême (attendance 210,000!).

These events are huge family affairs with civic receptions, great company, food, drink, and crowds, crowds, crowds, of academics, enthusiasts, serious students, ravers, housewives, superstars, mums and dads, school parties of wide-eyed kids; tons of ordinary people, all ages, all sexes, genuinely into comics. It has been a rare opportunity to feel normal, interesting and liked! (As a comics artist, I hasten to add. I mean I am all those things. Really!)

DAZE OF WHINING NEUROSES

If it seems like I'm blowing my own trumpet I'm not. I'm just so bloody relieved, is all.

Bien sûr, it's not all wine 'n' roses and the sheer contrast is liable to make my head spin (swell!), and my view hyperbolic. But ... it is like a *vision* of the way a comic-book life here could be, should be, but in all likelihood never will be. Our national culture is either too jaded or immature. We can't even look at Art without feeling shame and embarrassment, without worrying about trend, class, profit: Worrying we look stupid if we don't find the meaning, or a clever-clogs if we do, instead of reacting or not reacting and settling for that. We don't seem able to accept creative

telling stories of a calibre and character matched nowhere else in modern media. By comparison with much of it, what I'm doing is diverting fluff. The joke is that we are all virtually ignored because of a truly ignorant public perception of our chosen medium. And all I can do here is preach to the, presumably, already converted. All 2000 of you.

Stubbornly pursuing my own personal vision with this comic series has involved more personal sacrifice than I ever bargained for and even still no monetary gain. Hence the French edition has felt like a rubber ring thrown to a man waving and drowning. "Just fuck off and live in France then, eh?" If UKplc wasn't the very stuff of my stories, if my work wasn't just so British, I guess I would. For better or worse, for poorer and poorer, I live in Cool Britannia, and ♪ things can only get better♫ – for reasons entirely too ironic for this government to take credit for, except in the worst way.

The comics mainstream continues to thrash about in a tar-pit of nostalgia, but its suicide only serves to clear the way for the new blood, modestly camped in leftfield but on far safer ground. And somewhere in that no-man's-land in between, some ambitious folks are setting

The above cartoon was 'speciale pour *clin d'oeil*', <glimpse>, a freebie supplement available across france to all train passengers on SNCF. Imagine if you can a miniature version of *Comics International* being given away on British Rail! It appeared in the Janvier 99 Angoulême Special.

CAUSE CÉLÉBRE

Excerpts from some of the international press reviews of *Le CLUB de la fin de siècle*:

...Il suffit de lire les trois pages d'intro pour se rendre compte de l'énergie étonnante de ce jeune autuer. À la fois sec comme on vieux solo de batterie, élégant comme un ligne de basse funky et poignant comme un break de cuivres bien juteux...
L'affiche, Aout 1998

<you only have to read the first three pages to realize the astonishing energy of this young(!) author.> not entirely

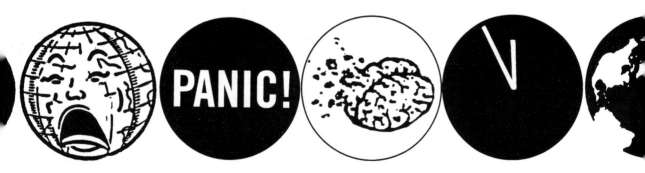

activity on its own terms - for what it is, as opposed to the image of it; obsessed with style as opposed to substance.

Surprisingly, there are a great many comics creators currently

up a brightly bannered marquee, organising Easter's Comics 99 event – on a somewhat European model.

Who knows what tomorrow may bring!

clear on the next bit but basically its a musical analogy... <At the same time dry as an old ... something ..., elegant like a funky bass line, and poignant (?) as a well-played drum break.>

The WORLD of THE END as we know it

Ilya, echte naam Ed Hillyer, is al een flinke tijd aktief in het Britse Small Press wereldje. Hij brengt regelmatig iets uit on werkt ook met/voor andere tekenaars als scenarist. Zijn laaste produkt heet "End of the Century", een essef

aprire un loro localino, sono gli elementi di un'avventura al fulmicotone che, visto il successo riscontrato, godra dal '98 di vita propria nell'albo The End.

Boutros-Boutros Ghali,
Channel 9 News

An <inevitable> (but happy!) comparison to The Full Monty, <...since it concerns itself with a group of friends searching for a way out of the poverty trap...>. Yes, the French love cinema. I would suggest to them the glib but

kortverhaal over 2 jongens die aan een verkeerslicht aan de slag komen als ramenlapper en krantenverkoper. Prima tekenwerk!!

Peter Van Laarhoven,
De Nieuwe Stripgids, Belgium.
(Uh, thanks. I think.)

The first six pages of book one have also been translated into Galician (a regional dialect comprehensible to both Spanish and Portuguese), in O Fanzine Das Xornadas Numero 3, Outubro de 1996; an excerpt to accompany a short article about it. Thanks to Henrique Torreiro of Colectivo Phanzynex.

Di produzione britannica e invece la graphic novel The End of the Century Club di Ed Hiller (alias Ilya), apparsa a puntate sulla rivista Deadline prima di venire raccolta in volume autoprodotto, subito esaurito, ora riveduto e ristampato da Panic!/Slab-O-Concrete: scampoli di cultura rave, devastanti concerti rock, organizzatori di gigs in combutta con repressive forze di polizia, umori urbani da fine millennio, grattacapi della gioventu on the dole con un manipolo di simpatici e squattrinati squatters che a tutti i costi vogliono

No actually: Vittore Baroni, Rumore, Novembre 1997 (an italian rock/style mag) Blimey, Italian sentences never end, just like when they talk! (Hi Giulia!)

...Inventif et drôle.
Jalouse, Sept 1998

<Inventive and droll.> Unsurprisingly. What is a surprise is that Jalouse is a slick chic French women's mag, yet!

...On pense immanquablement au film génial The Full Monty, puisqu'il s'agit d'une bande de copains qui cherchent une solution pour sortir de la misère...
Tout Meles

bizarre parallel La Haine meets Ma Vie En Rose, and in return they often tried to peg me alongside features from Brit cinema. Aside from Monty, mention was also made of Les Virtuouses <Brassed Off>, "same distancing humour, same outlook" (Technikart, Octobre 98), Ken Loach, and Trainspotting. I resisted this last one where I could since drugs don't really feature, pointing instead to the far superior Small Faces. Scotch, released around the same time, utterly brilliant. The director Gilles Mackinnon has since made Regeneration and Hideous Kinky, both films equally excellent and thoroughly recommended to anyone who loves a great story well told.

Barney and Tippoo go Galician

Barney and Tippoo en Français

Deanne dress-up dolly

by Lisa Canham

Deanne dress-up dolly by Lisa Canham of Norwich. "I like to think it kinda looks like Xo from Love'n'Rockets, (...or...) a swimsuit model from the 50's. She's not fat - just born in the wrong decade - always a good excuse!" And a great line - I'll take it! Lisa goes on to say, "as you will find I've tried to reproduce the outfits she wears in E.O.T.C. but I think you'll find she looks most resplendent in the Princess Leia Slave Girl costume!." Indeed. Try not to get too excited, reader! I only wish I could show you Lisa's superb gift in glorious full colour. Lisa works at Norwich's ABSTRACT SPROCKET comics emporium and has apparently made a mobile featuring the End Club gang for the shop. If you are in the vicinity (29 St Benedict's Street) check it out!

Exhibitions up against the wall, motherfucker

Pages from *The End* (25,26) appeared in exhibition as part of June 98's SHOCK event at the Gardner Arts Centre, Brighton; ostensibly to celebrate the work of Aubrey Beardsley (1872-1898), and marking the centenary of his death. The organisers Cartoon County asked artists to respond to the culture at the end of our century, as Beardsley did at the end of his. In a fit of artistic pique I had scrapped the original first 18 pages of *The End* #1. When I came to re-draw this scene ☚ I realised I had willy-nilly self-censored the depiction first time around : Why be so coy about showing Willie's willy? Gay sex scenarios aren't exactly common outside of 'It's-a-Gay-Comic' comics. In the spirit of Beardsley I could have taken things a lot further, and had it fit with the narrative probably would have. Maybe next time...

My other lurid (full colour) SHOCK entries featured Tank Girl and Booga in an enthusiastic '69', and Sonic the Hedgehog furiously buggering his little squirrel friend Tails, so you can tell I had fun. All this filth accompanied us on the Cartoon County weekender at the Darnétal festival in Normandy, France, where the kids were suitably spellbound, requesting a great many sketches of Sonic, *"comme ça"*. I duly obliged, if not quite <like that>. Meanwhile, the adolescents were solemnly transfixed (probably mentally recording the imagery for 'later').

The previous year to SHOCK, Cartoon County's exhibition was *The Cartoonist's Progress*, in honour of the 300th anniversary of the birth of William Hogarth, 1697-1764. It featured a page from *Nightshift* (so far unpublished). *End* artwork cropped up in the catalogue too, alongside this :

"Hogarth's England – A Selection of the Engravings (Folio Society, 1957) was in the house as I grew up. I don't know MUCH I looked at it then, but I guess some of it must have seeped in somewhere. Hogarth told 'stories with pictures' in an 'earthy and robust' manner. Likewise, my comic strips tend to deal with what could be broadly termed 'social politics': Petty theft and unemployment (Bic/Skidmarks): self-determination in UKplc (End of the Century): racism (Nimby): council estate loneliness and gentrification (The Hermit Crab): and polysexuality ('The Body', in 1997's It's Dark in London, *a noir anthology from Serpent's Tail). According to Horace Walpole, Hogarth 'wrote... a history of the manners of the age'. I can imagine no finer ambition, nor indeed example."*

During 1997-98, *The Cartoonist's Progress* toured far

and wide, from Gardner Arts to Swansea, via Crawley, Kidderminster, London's National Theatre, Kettering, Watford, Salford, and Santiago, Chile!

The last two weeks in October brought the CRISP comic art festival to Oxford Street and its environs. In addition to showing pages 78 and 136, I painted two (very) large *End* related artworks; a daffy Daddy Freddy (on a found shard of chipboard); and Willie and Tip as Shiva and Devi, proud parents of an infant Ganesa, ⬇ represented in this instance by a Californian elephant seal pup (being a prototype t-shirt design for

Migraine, a West Coast equivalent to Slab. This piece is an Indian cosmological equivalent of the Judeo-Christian immaculate conception, as enacted on the cover of *The End* 2 by the same imperfect couple. It will probably be the back cover of the French edition of this volume, pencilled in to appear in *Novembre 99*). ⬇

Pages 13, 14 and artwork from the *Nimby* Missive Device, all featuring nearby landmarks, were among the exhibits on show at The Clerk's House, Shoreditch ("an early Georgian building retaining many of its original features", and local to the Detonator studio, a.k.a. the CLUBhouse) for *Keen City*, July 22–Sept 6 1998. An electronic Arts newsgroup <londonart@dial.pipex.com> described it thus: *"The work on display has two things in common. Firstly, both good and bad aspects of urban life are reflected and, secondly, portrayed as 'Comic Art'; a product of popular culture, transformed into 'High Art' by the artists."* (...apparently...) *"Ilya's Bagels is an amusing portrayal of city workers' obsessions with consuming bagels at every opportunity."*

As I guess this goes to show, you take away what you bring to Art. One cream cheese tomato, one egg mayonnaise, and a Coke.

RecommENDed Reads

REPLACEMENT GOD
by Zander Cannon

One BIG collection and the self-same first eight issues published by Slave Labor/Amaze Ink. Volume 2, issues #1-5 published through Image, #6 onwards self-published. Current issue (6) is an 80-page monster, available from Handicraft Guild Studios, 89 S.10th street no. 315, Minneapolis, Minn. 55403. $6.95 + postage. If you liked the mediæval flavour of Barney's daydreams, you'll love this!

SKELETON KEY
by Andi Watson.

Four (count 'em) gorgeous collections and related back issues (1-30), plus upcoming new four-issue mini-series, all from Slave Labor. Also GEISHA, a four-ish mini from Oni Press. As Andi is the writer on the HOT comic incarnation of new teen-horror series *BUFFY the Vampire Slayer*, the dude is really beginning to go places(his *Buffy* scripts are good, but compared to his OWN comics, *Buffy* bites!). Get on board before the rush!

FINDER
by Carla Speed McNeil

$2.95, bi-monthly (and regular!), 13 issues to date. Indescribably excellent in every way possible. My brain's favourite food. Self-published by Lightspeed Press, P.O. Box 448, Annapolis Junction MD 20701 U.S.A. Slab has some early numbers, and there MUST be a collection planned (CSM?). Find it!

LOVEBOMB
by Paul B. Rainey

£2/$2.95, 2 issues so far, from Abaculus Press, 1 Bentall Close, Willen, Milton Keynes, MK15 9HB, UK. Abnormally good tales of the bizarre in the normal, and the normal in the bizarre. I mean, we're talking Milton Keynes here! Printed in the UK by YBE Business Forms Ltd. See what I mean?

SUGAR BUZZ
by Carney/Phoenix

7 issues and rising from Slave Labor again. Abnormally weird tales of the bizarre in the bizarre. All the Saturday morning cartoons you think you saw but never did, screened direct from the Id.

WORMWOOD
by Chris Webster

2 issues, everyone impatient for #3. And where's *Hopper and Fly*? £1.50 each from 13a Dulwich Rd., London SE15 0N7, UK . Also try the previous four issue MALUS for a bargainous £4. Jus' plain abnormal.

Also, watch for HUNDEGOTT (<Dog God>, and otherwise in English!) upcoming from DRONE's Danish Detonator Søren Mosdal. Decadent and disturbing goings on in Dada era Berlin which by all rights should make this lanky talent an international superstar. If they don't put him away first.

American viewers can reach Slave Labor toll free on 1-800-866-8929. In the UK shop at GOSH!, Page 45, Abstract Sprocket, Bristol's Forbidden Planet and any other good comic shops you can find. Curious retailers who want to invest in the future (and begin to do as well as these outfits) could do worse than contact indie distributors Red Route on 0181-960 5855, and request their excellent catalogue!

TO THE
END

Most of the material in this book collection first appeared as a four issue mini-series, THE END, available in more enlightened comics shops over the course of the last year. All of it is reprinted here plus plenty more besides, but if you want to see some pretty damn spiffy colour covers and editorial rants and whinges exclusive to these initial publications by all means (and you'll need to) search them out, or order direct from Slab. What follows are edited highlights from some of the letters of comment and e-mails recieved ...

"The End is the living end, man! Fast ,funny, funky, frivolous and foughtful."

Simon Russell, Peterborough

> Fanks.

"I think it is funny how Willie has the face of the ideal 50's man – albeit with dreadlocks."

Juniper Sage, Boulder, Colorado

"I don't know if The End is having any kind of impact. Maybe some people like me have put it to one side, thinking of reading the whole story all in one go. People with shot away memories who can't remember a storyline from one month (or whatever) to the next.

I laughed out loud several times, which doesn't happen often with many comics I read these days. Maybe once in a while you or your characters' weakness for a crap pun does seem a bit of an indulgence, but what the fuck... it's worth it for the good ones."

Dick Foreman, South Wales

> And everyone seems to have their own idea which the good ones are, which is why I guess I continue to indulge. My weakness for bad puns gets on even my wick sometimes. I almost overlarded this time out. What can I say? My Dad does it. My

stepbruv does it. I'm innocent, guv. Just a product of my environment.
Shot away memories ('What's in that cigarette'?) are related to at least one of the themes of the next major storyline, INFO SICK. *Unless I forget to include them.*

"**1** Pinpoint characterization; nuanced caricature; a great cast
2 Brisk storytelling; breakneck breakdowns; ingenious, fluid transitions
3 Eisneresque skill w/ layouts; varied surfaces
4 Deliberate & meaningful variations in style, rendering, tone values
5 Graphic energy, Kirbyesque kineticism
6 Droll humor; broad humor
7 Wicked suspense
8 Well-observed cultural milieu/ punk ethos
9 Sense of social urgency; political thrust
10 Elegant design; tip-top production
11 Organic capacity for growth, change and apt surprise
12 Thus, boundless potential for future volumes

... [a] rousing , full-throttle comic: Passionate and impeccably crafted: Studied but rowdy, frenetic and joyous."

> Wiz zis you are zpoiling uz. Zis 'dozen points o' praise' was posted on an alt.comix e-mail list by ambassador of comics Charles Hatfield, who then went on to furnish me with a scorching review in Comics Journal. *Thankyou, sir! If you've anything to say about this new book I'm all ears. Kudos also to Tom Furtwangler for downloading and forwarding the list to me. Any e-types who spot, or themselves post anything END related on the net, I really would appreciate it if you could do the same and wave it under my virtual nose. amazon.co.uk list End of the Century Club: COUNTDOWN on their at a glance book info. If anybody wants to review it there please do so.*

"It's odd to read in *Comics International* that you nearly didn't have enough orders to continue the series... [and then reading] about the latest tits-out extravaganza. I suppose coverage is coverage (!). And of course, Tippoo is far sexier than any of that tat. Something about a personality, perhaps?

Since I cycle to work, I was pleased to see Bic egging up his bike. Having been nearly run down a couple of weeks ago, I think that bricks would be a better option."

Stephen Prestage, Nottingham

>The typical car drivers' response to nearly killing someone is a curious mix of anger and accusation. Do they bluster reflexively to avoid culpability, clearly aware that they have done something wrong? It's like showing a naughty puppy-dog

the crap it's just done on the carpet only to have it turn and take your arm off... or insist that the turd is in fact one of yours. Or, stress pumped with road rage, do they simply not care? Showing more concern for their paintwork than the body whose blood is spattered across it – "LOOK WHAT YOU'VE DONE TO MY CAR!" – displays a stunning disregard for the welfare of fellow human beings; married with an unhealthy and probably Freudian attachment to their vehicle. Having said that, I love my bicycle. And have been known to get shirty with pedestrians who assume silent traffic equals no traffic.

I'm glad you think Tippoo is sexy, but doubt it is down to her personality, as such. At the start I thought it challenging to have a cute girl character who, as a person, was actually pretty unpleasant. Pretty/unpleasant. As I've got to know her, discovering reasons for her attitude and behaviour beyond belying her good looks, it has turned out less simplistic than that.

I was concerned that the 'arranged marriage' plotline was a trifle obvious, the stereotypical Anglo-Indian angle. Two people I know, one female, one male, happen to have gone through similar ordeals due to their cultural split. Though white, I live in a pre-dominantly Indian part of London. A group photograph of my family could be mistaken for a Benetton advert. And having taken pains to make my portrayal authentic, I myself am satisfied with the result. Stereotypes, often self-fulfilling, exist for a reason. If you disagree, I'm keen to hear your views (And I hope the crew at Page 45 and

their customers enjoyed the parallax view of Future Now Nottingham. Let me know!)

When sketching pin-ups or signing books the usual request is to draw Willie or Tip. Willie Tip, Willie Tip, all day long. It can get pretty tiring, you know! A few folks prefer Bic. A fondness for Skidmarks? (If you'll pardon..). And then there's the occasional hunky Buck in the buff. So predictable, for shame! I'm still waiting for someone to ask for Deanne, draped or undraped (Charlotte of Stratford wants to see her get a shag, though. Duly noted.) I don't know … you comics fans and your bad girls fixation!

These phantom pregnancies keep cropping up. Pic by Andi Watson

"Things that I particularly like about The End: Nothing much actually seems to be happening. Honest! I really,really like the fact that I had to wade through a whole book and most of a 64 page comic before the club even opened. Nice to see someone taking their time for a change. It

shows a real commitment to your story and characters.

You've taken a basically unlikeable bunch (a gay crusty, a comics nerd, an American, a babe with attitude, and , worst of all, A CYCLIST!) and made them sympathetic and likeable.

My only real complaint is that sometimes it seems that you're trying way too hard to get a point across, and this tends to leave the overall message a little heavy handed. With storytelling skills as strong as yours, you really don't need to belabour any points."

Rob Wells, London

> It's my firm intention to tackle this. I don't like 'message' stories. But, I suspect that if you're too clever a writer, a lot of the more casual readers (or those with shot away memories) miss or misinterpret stuff. Even so, in my bread-winning health education work I'm often encouraged to underestimate the readership, and instinctively resist it. The point is to invite interest and inspire attention, not dumb down. So, I try to layer the pleasures and rewards so that there's something for everyone - broad strokes, filigree inbetween. My own thought processes are fairly simple, if multifarious, and my speech can be blunt. And so I guess it is in my stories. Hopefully, even the passages of blinding polemic throw shadows that cast everything in a fuzzier light. Given that I am myself characterised by about 65 % of the attributes you dislike, and no doubt they cover a goodly proportion of the readership too, I was tempted, Rob, to run your full address...

Tippoo and Deanne "back from the hairdresser's just in time for the *End of the Century* 'Swimsuit Special'" pic by Lincoln pimp Dom Morris

"Before finding your book, tagged as 'recommended reading' in Forbidden Planet in Bristol, the nearest I'd got to graphic novels was seeing the film *Chasing Amy*.

Glad I did, though. Near future decay is easier to relate to than the far-future/other worlds scenarios in other non-mainstream books. We all dialled John Major's Collapse of Society Hotline a few years ago without result.

Last week I read Stephen Booth's *City Death*. He envisions even more brutal policing than you do. Actually, the police are one of my favourite features of *The End*. As an intermittent road-protestor and regular Reclaim The Streets attendee I've got a seat right by the catwalk for changing fashions in club (with riot shield) gear. Thames Valley Police this season are modelling a crash helmet ominously similar to what German soldiers wore in WW2 – pariculary the matt finish

which is a radical departure from traditional styling. I notice some of your security operatives wearing filter masks while others do not - creating the entertaining possibility of one unit deploying a chemical their competitors are unprotected from. A subversive publication reported an arguably more impressive bit of incompetence when an officer fired his CS spray into a headwind putting 12 of his chums out of action. To paraphrase Tom Lehrer: The force not only prohibits recruitment discrimination on grounds of height, creed or colour – but also on grounds of ability."

Smin, Bath

>*Thanks for your observations, 'Smin'. Your details have been passed on to the relevant authorities. Expect a visit from one of their loyalisers, soon. (chink, chink. Why thankyou, officer. Merely doing my duty as a good citizen.)*

The possibility you entertain makes me want to bring back the long arm of the gendarmerie to drag their knuckles menacingly, and after that last scene don't doubt that I will. I've fun with helium in mind. Talking of gas, I found myself downwind of some CS gas one evening last autumn, whilst innocently sat outside a Soho pub. Even at 50 yards remove, not pleasant. If headlines I've seen recently are true it has become a common mishap.

You have to ask yourself why the police are getting such an ostentatious and expensive makeover. The new riot gear has even been featured in recruitment ads in the daily press. Implicitly, the invitation to get tooled up is a tempting one, and

they don't mind being seen appealing to that urge. Heaven forfend the police should start to dis-criminate.

By the way, Smin, do you want Rob's address?

"There is an incredible eroticism in the work. Not just in the naked people scenes either, but in the relationship tensions as well. The eroticism is there in the clothing. I like fashion. Being a creative type I can't help it. I don't like catwalk fashion, but I like street fashions. Watching people in crowded streets, young and old, male and female, what looks nice, comfortable, comfortable and honest, and just plain stoopid! 'Pants Ant' in *Sugar Buzz* #2 got me all dizzy, as trousers are a particular favourite compulsion with me.

It's a good time to be around in comics, things are changing, with a new breed coming through. Yourself, *Wormwood*, *Sugar Buzz*, *Lovebomb* are all valuable in pushing the medium forward. There is so much to hold things back it's a pleasure that so few can push it forward."

John Welding, ex-*Goatherd*

> *Amen to that, brother.
As for the rest, I printed it just to embarrass you. Sorry, John. Tee-hee.*

>Here endeth the letters. If at all humanly possible, the END CLUB gang will return before Big Nothing in another instalment. No more comics, unfortunately. For economic reasons we are sticking with the book format from now on – albeit about half the size of this monster, lengthwise. I was worried I might be too big for you. Everything

and everyone is pretty much established and old plotlines resolved, so now the fun really begins! All I will say is at least one character will be waking up in the wrong bed (those compulsive trousers again!). I hope to run more letters next time out so do write in, and remember to include an address. Anyone whose comments I print or act upon will recieve (pot-luck) a full colour mini-comic, or poster, or sketch.

Less of a competition, which may involve all sorts of legal bollocks, more of a wee challenge (or three):

1) Within the first 48 pages (103-56) of *The END of the CENTURY CLUB: COUNTDOWN* there are 19 musical references (usually, but not always, lyrics) to various popular music combos of the day and/or their jolly humalong tunes. Some mainstream, some painfully obscure. Whoever writes in and identifies the most gets some original art. Even if you can only spot two or three you may still have a chance of winning, as let's face it less than a handful will probably bother in the first place!

2) There is a costume party at the CLUB. Who dresses up as what? If you are willing to do a little sketch or drawing of your suggestion(s), even better, but its the ideas that count. Same deal as above.

3) THE PARTY GUEST FROM HELL. What is the most evil trick you've had played on you, or the most anti-social thing you've ever done, at a house party? Rumour, popular myth and wicked flights of imagination allowed too. A future story idea involves acts of revenge and pure spite committed just so. All

nightmare party scenarios welcome, and rewards for anything I make use of.

And finally, one last letter - genuine, signed, craving my

indulgence, nay, begging for my vote (I recieved it almost the very day I turned 18.) The soliciting correspondant? A certain lady whose name you might recognise. Take it away, Ma'am...

---

10 DOWNING STREET

May 1986

Dear Edward Hillyer

I am writing to you because your name appears as a new elector in the latest Register of Electors for this constituency, Finchley. If you have recently come to live within the constituency, I am delighted to welcome you. (If you have simply moved address within the constituency, I apologise for troubling you, but I hope, nevertheless, that this letter proves helpful).

If there is any way you think I might be able to help you in my capacity as your Member of Parliament, do please write to me. For letters to reach me as quickly as possible, they should be sent to me at 10 Downing Street, London, SW1A 2AA and they should be marked "For the attention of the Constituency Secretary." I am regularly in the constituency and meet constituents who have a specific problem with which a Member of Parliament can help.

If you want any further information, please contact my Constituency Agent, Andrew Thomson. His office is at 212 Ballards Lane, Finchley, N3 2LX and his telephone number is ████████.

As your Member of Parliament, I represent all the constituents of Finchley, regardless of their political affiliation, and it is in this spirit that I am writing to you.

Yours sincerely

Margaret Thatcher

Edward Hillyer
56, Nether Street
London
N12 7NG

Other EDitions...

The END of the CENTURY CLUB

120 pgs • 185 x 260mm
ISBN: 0 9527386 0 0
£7.99 UK • $12.50 USA

Willie, Bic, Barney, Tippoo and Deanne come together after another party is bust by rival rent-a-cop outfits. Totally marginalised, they must create their own future whilst dodging workfare and local gangsters. The aim: to pull together a cafe-cum-club-cum-drop-out's-drop-in-centre, a space to stage the party to end all parties at the turn of the millennium.

A furious, rabble-rousing, hilarious and epic comic strip tale of bonding, bitching and bedlam, and an accurate and entertaining depiction of life on the edge in UK plc, as the Twentieth century gasps its last.

END of the CENTURY

20 pgs • A4 • £1 • $2
The invaluable 'prologue' to the series. Featuring Bic, Barney and even Spinner if you don't blink.

NIMBY

20 pgs • A6 • £1 • $2
2 colour mini-format comic with three colour cover. Bastard bone-dome in bovver boots and bomber jacket earns his karmic comeuppance!

Prices include postage inside the UK • Make cheques/POs payable to **Slab-O-Concrete**, PO Box 148, Hove, BN3 3DQ • overseas customers please add £1 per book and 50p per comic for postage and send well concealed cash, an IMO or add £5 to a cheque in your own currency for bank charges See our website at **www.slab-o-concrete.demon.co.uk** for other great titles